Ella Moves House

Angela Hassall

Illustrated by Caroline Ewen

Tamarind

ELLA MOVES HOUSE
TAMARIND BOOKS 978 1 848 53006 5

Published in Great Britain by Tamarind Books,
a division of Random House Children's Books
A Random House Group Company

This edition published 2010

1 3 5 7 9 10 8 6 4 2

TAMARIND BOOKS
61–63 Uxbridge Road, London, W5 5SA

www.tamarindbooks.co.uk
www.kidsatrandomhouse.co.uk
www.rbooks.co.uk

Addresses for companies within The Random House Group Limited can be found at: www.randomhouse.co.uk/offices.htm

THE RANDOM HOUSE GROUP Limited Reg. No. 954009

A CIP catalogue record for this book is available from the British Library.

Printed and bound in China

For Natasha, Rebecca, Oscar, India & Isabel
Also for Ella
A.H.

For Oscar and Poppy
Also for Peter
C.E.

Ella and her mum live in a flat in a big city.
The flat is just the right size for Ella and her mum.
There is room for Ella's animal friends and Mollie the doll.

Mollie is Ella's very special friend.
She sleeps in the doll's house with the broken door.
It is just the right size for her.

Ella's mum has a very special friend too.
His name is Joe. Joe can do lots of things.
He can jump and sing and fly a kite.
He can play the guitar and juggle with doughnuts.
He makes Ella's mum laugh.
But he does not make Ella laugh.

Joe swings Ella round and round.
"Put me down," she shouts. "PUT ME DOWN.
I AM GOING TO BE SICK."

"Let's catch leaves," cries Joe.
"No," says Ella. "It is too blowy."

"Splish! Splosh! Let's jump
in the puddles," laughs Joe.
"No, I don't want to," says Ella.
"IT IS WET."

"See the kite fly," shouts Joe.

"No," says Ella.
"Kites are silly."

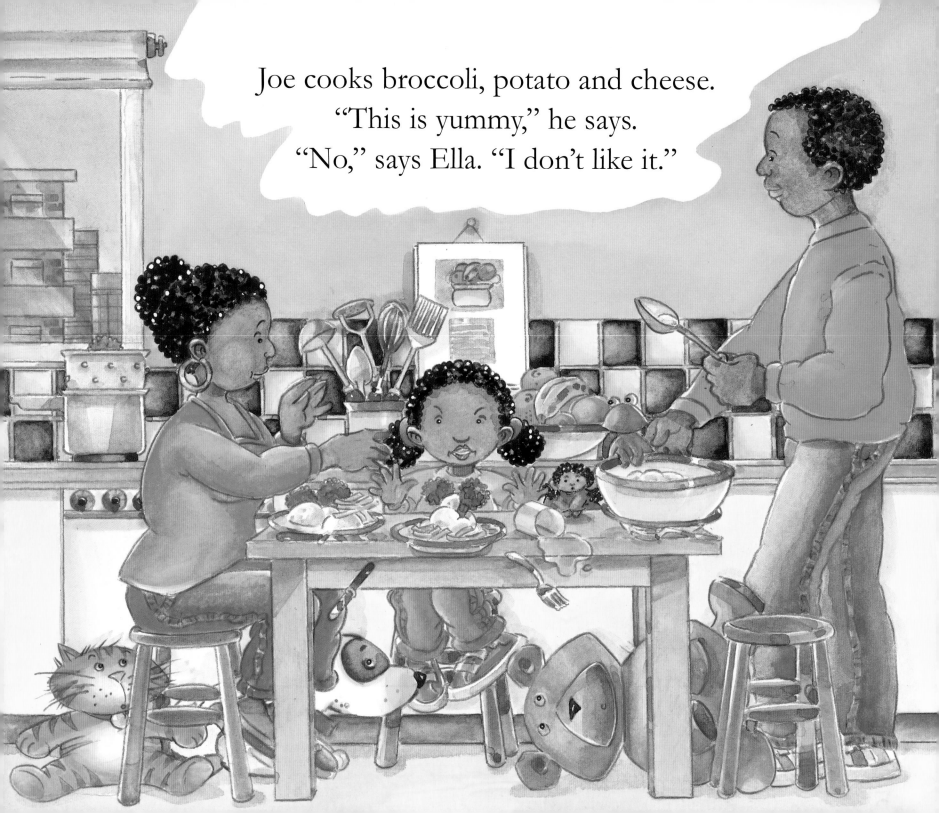

Joe cooks broccoli, potato and cheese.
"This is yummy," he says.
"No," says Ella. "I don't like it."

Joe and Ella's mum sit on the sofa and watch TV.
Ella wants to watch TV too.
But there is no room on the sofa.
She wants to play with her toys.
But there is no room on the floor.
Not any more.

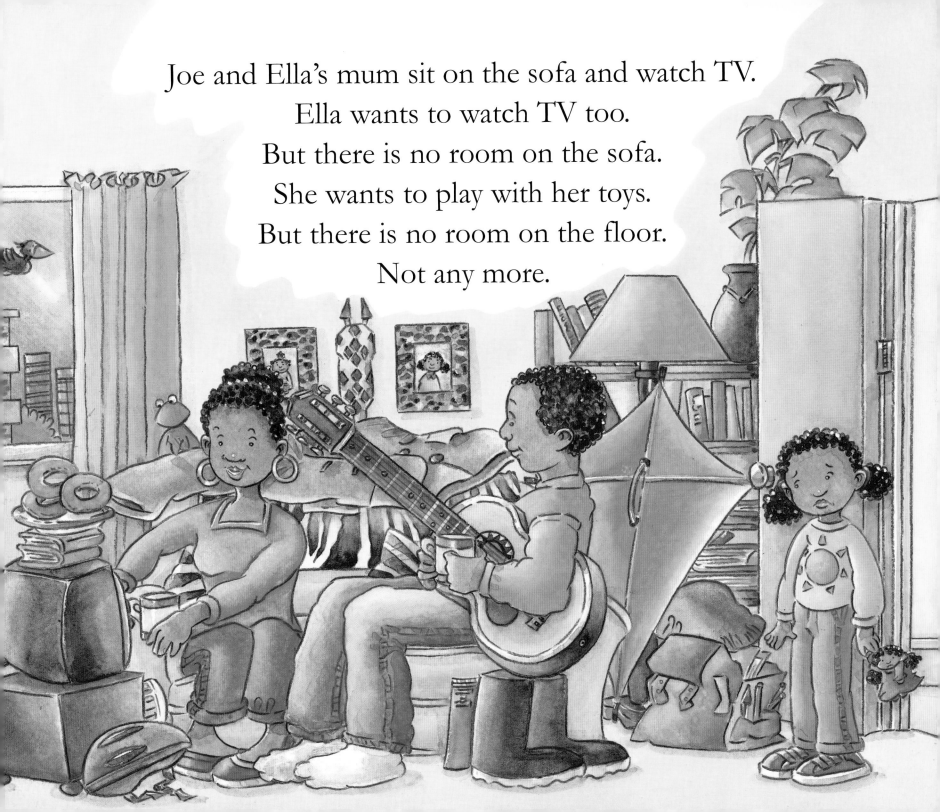

"We are going to a new house tomorrow,"
says Ella's mum. "This place is too small."
"All of us?" asks Ella. "You and me and the animals and Mollie?"
"Yes," says Ella's mum. "And Joe."

"No!" says Ella. "I don't want Joe and
I don't want to go to a new house."
"Don't be silly," says Ella's mum. "Of course you do."
"NO! I DON'T!"

"Wrap up Mollie and your animal friends,"
says Ella's mum. "Pack them in this box for the move."
"But they don't want to be packed up," says Ella.

"Yes they do," says Ella's mum.
"No they don't!" says Ella.
"And Mollie does not like sleeping in boxes.
She only likes sleeping in her house."

But Ella's mum and Joe wrap up Mollie and
the animals and pack them in the cardboard box.
Ella watches.

That night when Ella's mum and Joe are in the kitchen
Ella gets out of bed and creeps along the hallway.

She stands quite, quite still by the living room door and waits…
until her mum and Joe are busy.

Then… she tiptoes into the living room and
opens the box. Quiet as a mouse
she takes Mollie out and
puts her back in the doll's house.
"Good night, Mollie," she whispers. "Sleep tight."

The next morning Ella's mum and Joe carry
huge boxes out of the flat.
They put everything into the back of a big van
and slam the doors shut. Ker-bang!

They all climb in.
"Here we go," says Joe. "Toodle-oo."
Joe starts to sing. Ella's mum sings too.

If you're happy and you know it, clap your hands...
If you're happy and you know it,
and you really want to show it...
If you're happy and you know it,
clap your hands!

"Sing along, Ella," says Joe.
"No," says Ella. "I don't want to sing and
I don't like new houses."

At the new house
Mum and Joe unload everything and carry it in.
Joe unloads the doll's house.

But something is wrong…
The door of the doll's house is wide open.
"Mollie's gone," wails Ella. "Oh, where is she?"

"Safe in the box," says Ella's mum.
"No she is not," sobs Ella. "I took her out.
I put her back in her house."

"Don't cry, Ella," says Joe. "Have a doughnut."
"I don't want a doughnut, I want Mollie," shouts Ella.
The biggest dog in the whole world races up.

"Look," says Ella's mum. "Look at that dog."
The big dog bounces and pounces on something…

"Mollie!" Ella screams.
The big dog shakes Mollie and growls.
"PUT MOLLIE DOWN!" shrieks Ella.

But the dog jumps over the fence into a garden.
"Stop thief!" shouts Joe.
He jumps over the fence after the dog.

SOLD

The dog jumps into the next garden. Joe jumps too.
The dog leaps over a garden gate.

Joe leaps over the garden gate…

and catches the dog!
"Have a doughnut," says Joe to the dog.
"Go on, have two. They are yummy!"

The dog wags its tail, drops Mollie,
gobbles up the doughnuts and gallops off.

"Here you are, Ella," says Joe. Ella hugs Mollie tight.
"Thank you, Joe," she says. "Oh, thank you, thank you!"

"You are welcome. Fancy a twirl?"
"I do. Oh yes, I do."
Joe swings her round and round, round and round.
Ella laughs and laughs.

"When are you two coming into the house?" shouts Ella's mum.
"Right now," says Joe.

"Right now," shouts Ella. "I like new houses."
Joe and Ella go into the new house together,
hand in hand.

OTHER TAMARIND TITLES

FOR *Ella Moves House* READERS

Why Can't I Play?
Danny's Adventure Bus
Siddharth and Rinki
My Big Brother JJ
Big Eyes, Scary Voice
North American Animals
South African Animals
Caribbean Animals
What Will I Be?
Choices, Choices…
All My Friends
A Safe Place
Dave and the Tooth Fairy
The Night the Lights Went Out
Mum's Late

BOOKS FOR OLDER READERS

The Day the Rains Fell
Amina and the Shell
The Silence Seeker
The Feather
The Bush
Marty Monster
Starlight
Boots for a Bridesmaid
Yohance and the Dinosaurs
The Dragon Kite
Princess Katrina and the Hair Charmer

To see the rest of our list
please visit our website:

www.tamarindbooks.co.uk